Dear Parents and Educators,

Welcome to Penguin Young Readers! As parents and educators, you know that each child develops at his or her own pace—in terms of speech, critical thinking, and, of course, reading. Penguin Young Readers recognizes this fact. As a result, each Penguin Young Readers book is assigned a traditional easy-to-read level (1–4) as well as a Guided Reading Level (A–P). Both of these systems will help you choose the right book for your child. Please refer to the back of each book for specific leveling information. Penguin Young Readers features esteemed authors and illustrators, stories about favorite characters, fascinating nonfiction, and more!

Young Cam Jansen and the Lost Tooth

LEVEL **3**

GUIDED READING LEVEL **J**

This book is perfect for a **Transitional Reader** who:
- can read multisyllable and compound words;
- can read words with prefixes and suffixes;
- is able to identify story elements (beginning, middle, end, plot, setting, characters, problem, solution); and
- can understand different points of view.

Here are some **activities** you can do during and after reading this book:
- Make Predictions: Pretend you are helping Cam solve the mystery. On page 20, Cam closes her eyes and pictures Annie wearing a smock when she lost her tooth. Cam thinks the tooth is in the pocket of the smock, but it's not. Now it is your turn—try to predict where you think the lost tooth is.
- Compare/Contrast: Cam is the main character in the story. Annie is the girl who Cam tries to help. Make a list of words that describe each of these characters. How are they alike? How are they different?

Remember, sharing the love of reading with a child is the best gift you can give!

—Bonnie Bader, EdM, and Katie Carella, EdM
  Penguin Young Readers program

*Penguin Young Readers are leveled by independent reviewers applying the standards developed by Irene Fountas and Gay Su Pinnell in *Matching Books to Readers: Using Leveled Books in Guided Reading*, Heinemann, 1999.

For Charles, Jared, Jeremy, Max, Yoni, Zev,
and, of course, Eitan—DA

To Colleen and Brenna Quinn—SN

Penguin Young Readers
Published by the Penguin Group
Penguin Group (USA) Inc., 375 Hudson Street, New York, New York 10014, USA
Penguin Group (Canada), 90 Eglinton Avenue East, Suite 700, Toronto, Ontario M4P 2Y3, Canada
(a division of Pearson Penguin Canada Inc.)
Penguin Books Ltd., 80 Strand, London WC2R 0RL, England
Penguin Group Ireland, 25 St. Stephen's Green, Dublin 2, Ireland (a division of Penguin Books Ltd.)
Penguin Group (Australia), 250 Camberwell Road, Camberwell, Victoria 3124, Australia
(a division of Pearson Australia Group Pty. Ltd.)
Penguin Books India Pvt. Ltd., 11 Community Centre, Panchsheel Park, New Delhi—110 017, India
Penguin Group (NZ), 67 Apollo Drive, Rosedale, Auckland 0632, New Zealand
(a division of Pearson New Zealand Ltd.)
Penguin Books (South Africa) (Pty.) Ltd., 24 Sturdee Avenue,
Rosebank, Johannesburg 2196, South Africa

Penguin Books Ltd., Registered Offices: 80 Strand, London WC2R 0RL, England

Text copyright © 1997 by David A. Adler. Illustrations copyright © 1997 by Susanna Natti. All rights
reserved. First published in 1997 by Viking and in 1999 by Puffin Books, imprints of Penguin Group
(USA) Inc. Published in 2011 by Penguin Young Readers, an imprint of Penguin Group (USA) Inc., 345
Hudson Street, New York, New York 10014. Manufactured in China.

The Library of Congress has cataloged the Viking edition
under the following Control Number: 96047357

ISBN 978-0-14-130273-7   10 9 8 7 6 5 4

Young Cam Jansen
and the Lost Tooth

by David A. Adler
illustrated by Susanna Natti

Penguin Young Readers
An Imprint of Penguin Group (USA) Inc.

Contents

Chapter 1
Cam Jansen Is Not Silly

"Gobble, gobble,"

Cam Jansen said.

She held up her turkey stick-puppet.

Eric Shelton smiled.

"When my puppet is finished,

our turkeys can be friends," he said.

Cam and her friend Eric

were sitting at Table Four in art class

with Annie and Robert.

It was almost Thanksgiving.

On the table were papers, crayons,

glue, scissors, string, beads,

and feathers.

There were also bowls

of apples and popcorn.

Robert said,

"Playing with paper turkeys is silly."

"It's fun, not silly," Cam said.

Eric told Robert,

"Cam Jansen is not silly!

She has an amazing memory.

Cam remembers everything she sees."

Robert said, "I don't think so.

No one remembers everything."

Cam looked at the necklace

Annie was making.

Cam closed her eyes and said,

"Click."

"Why did you say that?" Robert asked.

"My memory is like a camera,"

Cam told him.

"I have a picture in my head

of everything I have seen.

Click! is the sound

my camera makes."

"I don't think so," Robert said again.

Cam smiled.

Her eyes were still closed.

"The beads on Annie's necklace

8

are yellow, blue, red, red . . ."

"You're peeking," Robert said.

Cam turned around and went on,

". . . green, blue, white, black,

red, red, blue, and green."

"You're right!" Robert said.

"You do have an amazing memory."

Cam's real name is Jennifer.

But because of her great memory,

people started to call her

"the Camera."

Then "the Camera" became

just "Cam."

"My necklace is done,"

Annie said.

She put it on.

Then Annie took an apple

from the bowl.

She bit into it.

"Oh!" Annie screamed.

"Oh! My tooth!"

Chapter 2
My Tooth Is Gone

Annie ran to the sink.

Eric ran with her.

He gave Annie a cup of water.

Annie washed out her mouth.

Then Eric gave her a paper towel.

Annie held the towel to her mouth

and returned to the table.

"You're lucky," Robert told her.

"I lost a tooth once.

I put it under my pillow.

When I woke up, I found money there."

Annie took the towel from her mouth.

"That happens in my house, too,"

she said.

Annie looked in the paper towel.

She ran to the sink

and looked there, too.

Then she came back to the table.

"My tooth is gone," she said.

Mr. Fay, the art teacher,

took the large bell off his desk.

He rang the bell.

Ding! Ding! Ding!

"It's cleanup time," he called out.

Cam put the crayons in the box.

Eric put the feathers away.

Robert picked up the scraps of paper.

He put them in the recycling bag.

Annie was under the table.

She was looking for her tooth.

Mr. Fay came to Table Four.

"You did good work," he said.

"Thanks," Cam, Eric, and Robert said.

Mr. Fay picked up Cam's and Eric's

turkey stick-puppets.

"These look almost real."

He shook Cam's puppet and said,

"Gobble."

He shook Eric's puppet and said,

"Gobble, gobble."

Then he put the puppets down

and went to another table.

Cam and Eric picked up the beads.

"Hey," Eric said.

"These white beads look like teeth.

Annie's tooth must be in this box."

Annie crawled out from under

the table.

Eric and Annie

looked through the box of beads.

But they didn't find Annie's tooth.

Chapter 3
Click!

Cam, Eric, and Annie
gave their smocks to Robert.
He took them to the closet
and hung them up.
Mr. Fay rang the bell again.
Ding! Ding! Ding!
"It is time to go back to class,"
he said.
"Have a happy Thanksgiving."

Children from the other tables

walked out of the art room.

But Annie said, "I can't go back!

I still don't have my tooth."

"Don't worry," Eric told her.

"Cam and I will help you.

We will find your tooth.

We are good at finding things.

We are good at solving mysteries."

Cam closed her eyes.

She said, "Click!"

She said, "Click!" again.

Then she opened her eyes.

"I know where to find your tooth.

Come with me," Cam said.

Cam went to the closet.

Annie, Eric, and Robert followed her.

Ding! Ding! Ding!

Mr. Fay rang the bell again.

"You should be on your way to class,"

he said.

"Oh, Mr. Fay," Annie said.

"I lost my tooth."

Cam said, "And I know where to

find it."

Cam closed her eyes.

"Click!

I am looking at a picture

I have in my head.

It is a picture of Annie

when she lost her tooth.

She was wearing an art smock

with a big front pocket.

I think Annie's tooth

fell into the pocket."

Annie found her smock.

She reached into the pocket.

She took out two beads

and a feather.

"What else is in there?" Cam asked.

"Nothing," Annie answered.

There were tears in her eyes.

"I still don't have my tooth."

Chapter 4
Wake Up, Cam!

Cam, Eric, Annie, and Robert
left the art room.

Robert said, "I didn't think
you could say, 'Click,'
and find a tooth."

The children went into
their classroom.

It was quiet reading time.

Cam opened her book.

But she did not read.

She was thinking about Annie's tooth.

Cam closed her eyes and said, "Click!"

"Please, read quietly,"

the teacher said.

Cam whispered, "Click."

She sat for a long time

with her eyes closed.

Rrrr! Rrrr!

The school bell rang.

It was time to go home.

"Wake up, Cam! Wake up!" Eric said.

"It's time to go home."

Cam opened her eyes.

"I was not sleeping.

I was thinking about Annie's tooth.

But I don't know where it is."

Eric said, "We have to get our coats and lunch boxes.

We have to get on the bus."

Cam looked at Eric.

"Lunch boxes!" Cam said.

She closed her eyes.

"Click!"

Cam quickly opened her eyes.

"That's it!

I know where to find Annie's tooth.

Annie! Annie!" Cam called.

"We have to go to the art room."

Chapter 5
Here's Your Tooth

Eric took his coat and Cam's coat
from the closet.

He took their lunch boxes, too.

Cam and Annie were in the hall.

"Wait for me!" Eric called.

"Come on, Annie," Robert said.

"Let's go to the bus."

"Not now," Annie told him.

"We are going to get my tooth."

Robert shook his head and said,

"I don't think so."

Then he went outside to the bus.

Cam, Eric, and Annie

went to the art room.

Mr. Fay was carrying garbage cans.

"Wait!" Cam called out.

Cam reached into the garbage can

from Table Four.

She took out an apple.

Only one bite was missing.

"This was your apple," Cam said.

"And here is your tooth."

Cam gave Annie the apple.

"Thank you!" Annie said to Cam.

Annie took the tooth out of the apple.

She put it in a paper towel.

Annie put the towel in her pocket.

Cam told Annie,

"Eric helped me find your tooth.

When he said 'lunch boxes,'

I thought about eating.

When I thought about eating,

I thought about the apple.

That's when I knew

where to find your tooth."

Annie thanked Eric.

Eric gave Cam her lunch box.

"Hurry or we will miss our bus."

Cam, Eric, and Annie ran outside.

The bus was still there.

"I wanted to leave," the driver said.

"But Robert asked me to wait."

Cam, Eric, and Annie thanked them.

Annie told Robert,

"Cam clicked and found my tooth."

Robert smiled.

"I knew she would find it!" he said.

A Cam Jansen Memory Game

Take another look at the picture on page 7.
Study it.
Blink your eyes and say, "Click!"
Then turn back to this page
and answer these questions:

1. How many children are there
   in the picture?

2. Is Cam smiling?

3. What's in the green and yellow bowl?

4. What color is the body of Cam's
   paper turkey? What color are
   its feathers?

5. Is there a jar of glue on the table?